Don't Let Ted Have Bubble Gum!

Written by Phyllis Armelie Sibbing

Illustrations by Cynthia Fisher

STECK-VAUGHN
COMPANY

A Division of Harcourt Brace & Company

This is my brother Ted.
He likes bubble gum.
Ted says he is the best at blowing bubbles.
He thinks bubble gum is fun.

One day I was at my desk.
Ted wanted me to see a big bubble.
All of a sudden, it went **POP!**

The gum was stuck in my hair.
"Ted, I will never get this gum out!" I yelled.

Bubble gum is no fun!

I said I was going to tell Mom.
"I will help you, Tess," said Ted.
"Let's try to brush it out."

I gave the brush a tug.
"Now I have gum in my hair AND in my brush," I said.

Bubble gum is no fun.

"I know what will help," said Ted.
"Let's get Mom's dusting powder.
 We can rub the gum out."

Ted put the dusting powder in my hair.
The gum was still stuck.
"Now my hair will be white!" I yelled.

Bubble gum is no fun.

"I know what will help," said Ted.
"Let's get the peanut butter."
Then he put a bunch on the gum.

Yuck! I looked like I had mud in my hair.
I smelled like dusting powder AND
peanut butter.

Bubble gum is no fun.

"Don't give up," said Ted.
"I know what will help.
 Let's scrub it out."

Ted told me to get in the tub.
He began to scrub.
He made too many suds!
Then my dress got wet!

Bubble gum is NO fun!

Just then Mom came in.
She saw the mess.
She did not yell.
All she said was "Get some ice."

The ice got some of the gum out.
The rest was still stuck.
Mom said, "Well, Tess, I think we must cut
your hair."

"Mom, please don't cut my hair," I begged.
Mom said it would be all right.
She gave me a big hug and began to cut.
My gummy hair fell to the floor.

Then Mom was done.
I spun around and looked in the mirror.
"I like it, Mom!
This is such a nice cut.
But please don't let Ted have bubble gum!"